Sore Loser

Sore Loser

By GENEVIEVE GRAY

Illustrated by Beth and Joe Krush

1974

HOUGHTON MIFFLIN COMPANY BOSTON

Library of Congress Cataloging in Publication Data

Gray, Genevieve S
    Sore loser.

    SUMMARY: Loren's difficult adjustment to a new
school is chronicled in various letters, school announce-
ments, and miscellaneous communiqués.
    [1. School stories]   I. Krush, Beth, illus.
II. Krush, Joe, illus.   III. Title.
PZ7.G7774So   [Fic]   73–22056
ISBN 0–395–18589–0

To Connie

Villa Verde Apartments, #27
14 Melville Place
Canfield Heights, California
March 20

Dear Mark,

Splashdown! Da-DAAAAAAAAAA!

I guess you're surprised to be hearing from me this soon. Well, Mom and I didn't expect to find a place to live this soon either, but here we are. We only looked at apartments where they took pets, so right away that cut out 90 per cent of the shopping around. This place is two blocks from my school and about a mile from Mom's new office.

Mr. Clean has already found a girl friend in the neighborhood only she is twice as big as he is and ugly as mud. I don't know what he sees in her. She is an evil companion teaching him bad habits. He is not white any more but black-and-white speckled. The two of them got into some oil some-where, only it doesn't show on her. She is black-

1

and-gray striped with an orange neck and one orange ear. Really weird.

Tonight Mom and I are going to organize the kitchen. We have a system. I unpack and she puts away.

Chow for now,
Loren

* * *

Dear Onyer Mark,

   *Mom went with me to sign up at school this
morning and I stayed for the day. The name of the
school is Willow Valley School. It looks like a
movie set, but that's California for you. Our school
in Oregon is dumpier, but I liked it better. At least
so far.*

   *Mom and I talked to the principal. He is a John
Wayne type named Mr. Wheeler. I guess he has
lots of problems, one being that he has to take kids
like me late in the year whether he wants to or not.
He looked at me like Geronimo wondering how
my scalp would look hanging on a pole. Mom tried
to thaw him out. She kept telling him (smile) how
sorry she was that the company transferred her in
March instead of August (smile), but she really
couldn't help it (smile). Geronimo finally smiled
back, but his heart wasn't in it.*

   *The kids here are okay I think, but after only one
day it's hard to tell. There are three 6th grades. I*

3

got Mrs. Ault's room. Mrs. Ault wears drip-dry knits and says *childring* instead of *children*. She's okay, but nothing like Miss Stewart. Tell Miss Stewart hi.

This is a bigger school than at home. I made a map so I wouldn't get lost.

There is a guy in my class, Bob Stevens. He is really okay. Man, can he shoot baskets. The other kids talked to me and showed me where stuff was. Maybe I'll get to know Bob Stevens better.

So long,
Loren

* * *

LOREN

Dear Mr. Wheeler,

I am returning Loren Ramsey's transfer record for the files. I am glad to have him.

Loren asked to join the school patrol, but Mrs. Barkeley told him to wait until next year. She has all the patrols she needs just now.

Helen Ault

* * *

STUDENT TRANSFER RECORD
MINTON (OREGON) SCHOOL DISTRICT
Elementary Grades

NAME: Loren Schuler Ramsey FATHER: (divorced)

ADDRESS: 4510 E. Heath Ave. MOTHER: Mrs. Karen Ramsey

SCHOOL: Harvey Robertson Elementary School

	Grade 1	Grade 2	Grade 3	Grade 4	Grade 5	Grade 6
Reading	A	A	A	A	A	(A)
Language	A	A	A	A	A	(A)
Science	A	A	A	A	A	(A)
Arith.	B	B	B	C	B	(B)
Art	A	A	A	B	A	(B)
Music	B	B	B	B	B	(B)
Citizenship	A	A	A	A	A	(A)

TEACHER COMMENT: Pupil withdrawn from school March 16.
Loren has been a wonderful pupil. We will miss him.

6th Grade Teacher
Melissa Stewart

* * *

Dear Mark,

Have you got my address? Why haven't you written me yet?

There's a big Science Fair coming up at school. From all the activity, it must be a big deal. The kids are working on their projects, and you never saw such an uptight bunch. Mrs. Ault says the childring must work on their own projects with no help from anybody. If one of the childring is caught getting help, he is exiled to Siberia. One guy here has a project that looks like a three-year-old did it, but Mrs. Ault is making him enter it in the Science Fair anyway.

"If he wants a better project, he'll have to work harder," she said.

I said, "Maybe he'd do better if somebody

8

showed him how." I tried to tell her how Miss Stewart had us do projects in Minton, but she didn't like it. "That's cheating," she said. "It's every pupil's responsibility to find out on his own," and she looked at me real hard. She may as well have gone ahead and said, ". . . and let that be a warning to you, buster!" because that's what she meant.

I don't get it. Not that I need all that much help. Still, if the kids are supposed to find out on their own, what's Mrs. Ault doing there? Miss Stewart let everybody help everybody else and we learned a lot more. Miss Stewart said sloppy work never taught anybody anything. Oh well.

Anyway I told Mrs. Ault about my rock collection, and she said I could use it since I got it together myself. I may have to switch though. Last night I looked for the box with my specimens, but no luck.

The moving van brought the rest of our stuff yesterday, and it looks like a refugee camp around here. My bed is stacked up with curtains. Mr.

Clean and I crawled under them last night and went to sleep anyway. I figured the curtains would never know the difference.

Please write to me.

Your old buddy,
Loren

* * *

Dear Ricky,

   Mother says I can have my
birthday party Saturday. All
the kids in the room are coming,
but Mother said I didn't have
to invite that stuck-up new
boy. He would only boss
everybody and argue with
Bob as usual. Please come
if you can. It will start
at two and last till five.

                    Emily

                * * *

The following Children will
sit at the Magazine Table
until they <u>Settle down.</u>

BETH HALSEY

SYLVIA MORSE

LOREN RAMSEY

TOM KENT

* * *

12

Dear Katherine,

Would you mind making up the schedule for our 6th grade softball games? Team captains from my room are Bob Stevens and Donnie Wheatley. They have chosen their teams, and we are ready to begin whenever you and Ellen are.

I have a new pupil, Loren Ramsey. So far he is a "square peg" and isn't adjusting very well. Can he keep score?

Helen Ault

* * *

Dear Sis,

My job is great and Loren and I are settled at last in the apartment, but that's the extent of the good news. We suffered a tragedy in the move. Loren's rock collection is gone. We've looked everywhere, but it seems to have just disappeared.

Loren is so disappointed he's speechless. Stares at the wall. I've filed a claim with the company, but the money won't help much. All the money in the world won't get Grandpa Ramsey's Plymouth Rock chip back, but there are other specimens just as difficult to replace. One of the most interesting ones was that glassy-looking shard Loren picked up in the gorge at Grand Canyon last summer. It's a sample of the oldest exposed rock anywhere in the world and Loren prized it. But the claim money certainly won't pay for a return trip to Grand Canyon!

On top of the rock collection loss, I'm beginning to suspect Loren hasn't found the going all that easy at school. Normally I'd expect him to steam like a tea kettle about his new friends and new plans, but so far not a word. I suspected maybe he'd been boasting too much about school at Minton and his exploits there. When I asked, he denied it so strongly I was sure I'd touched a sensitive spot. Loren can seem stuffy sometimes. He likes to claim he's "helping" people, but to others the "help" seems more like a put down.

I suppose his troubles will straighten themselves out in time, whatever they are. They always have in the past.

Saturday I was determined to at least give him something new to think about. We went exploring and happened on a deserted strip of beach about three miles from the apartment. We dashed home, made a picnic lunch, loaded up the cats, and returned to enjoy the ocean. ("Cats" — note plural. I refer to Mr. Clean and his companion, the stray I wrote you about.)

What a wonderful day it turned out to be! We took off our shoes and waded in the surf hunting wee beasties. *We chased waves and adventured up the nearby rocks with the cats. Loren had fun, I think. It was good to see him smile for a change.*

If you see Mark, please ask him to write to Loren. Mark's letters and the cats are all he seems to care about.

Love,
Karen

* * *

April 13

Dear Mrs. Ramsey,

When you moved in two weeks ago, you told me you only had one cat, but I see you have two. I must point out that your lease says tenants are limited to one pet each. You will have to get rid of the extra cat.

Arnold Lutkin, Manager
Villa Verde Apartments

* * *

April 4

Dear Mr. Lutkin,

I'm sorry the apartment office was closed when I got home from work, and I could not talk to you about the cats. I told you the truth about our pet. We have only one cat, Mr. Clean. He is a young, pure white male. We don't know where the other cat came from or to whom she belongs. In fact, I was under the impression she belonged to you and Mrs. Lutkin and was friendly with her on that account.

The extra cat seems to have adopted Mr. Clean and would like to adopt Loren and me, too. She guards us jealously from salesmen who come to the door and even snarled at the Welcome Wagon lady who was at first afraid to come into our apartment.

I haven't really tried to break the cat's habit of coming to our place, but after this word from you, I will. She has an astonishing appetite and would eat the upholstery, I believe, if we let her. I pity her real owner.

Now that we no longer believe the stray cat to be yours, your feelings won't be hurt if I tell you Loren calls her Old Melon-Head. (She is not a very pretty cat.) The cat now answers to Melon-Head or Mel. This information might be helpful in case she turns up at your place during the day when both Loren and I are away.

Sincerely yours,

Karen Ramsey

* * *

WILLOW VALLEY ELEMENTARY SCHOOL
TEACHERS' BULLETIN

April 5

Preparations for the Science Fair

It is good to see so many fine projects coming along in the classrooms. The janitors will have tables set up in the gym by noon, Wednesday, April 7. Pupils can begin putting up their exhibits Wednesday afternoon. Judging of exhibits will take place between 4 P.M. and 6 P.M. on Thursday. Dr. Levine will bring a team of judges from the university. Classes will be dismissed early on Friday to allow the children to attend the fair with their parents.

Albert Wheeler,
Principal

* * *

April 10

Dear Mark,

I was sure glad to get your letter today. Thanks for telling me about the gang. Tell Robin it's great about his new mini-bike.

At school yesterday they had the Science Fair, and man, what a drag. Thank goodness Mrs. Brooks let me spend most of the time in the library with her. The other kids' parents came by the zillion, but, of course, Mom couldn't. I guess it was just as well. One look at my project and she'd have broken out in hives. It was pretty bad, but not because I didn't try.

Mark, since you are my best friend, I'm going to tell you something I've decided. From this day henceforth, forevermore, I'm going to be extra nice to new kids — new at school, new in the neighborhood. Like that. Man, it's sure an all-gone feeling when there just isn't anyplace you can fit in. It's like going down fast in an elevator only worse because the feeling doesn't stop after a couple of minutes, but goes on all day, every day.

Take my advice. Don't ever move if you can help it. It's murder.

Mr. Clean and Mel are about the same. Mel still thinks Mr. Clean is her baby and tries to drag him around even though he's getting bigger all the time and so is she. She picks him up by the neck when she can catch him and gives him baths. The reason we named him Mr. Clean was because he spent so much time washing himself, but now he has old Mel baby to do all the work. She eats all his cat food, too, if we don't watch. We aren't supposed to feed her.

We still don't know who she belongs to, and I keep asking the neighbors hoping I'll find out. No luck yet. The manager told us we could only have one cat, and he said we had to get rid of Mel. Some joke. She sneaks into the apartment before I can grab her and hides. If I wait long enough though, I always know where to find her. There's a rag box in my closet full of old ripped-up towels and sheets. (Mom never throws anything away if she can help it.) Mel found it the second day we were here and staked it out as her private territory. She won't even let Mr. Clean in the box with her.

When she's in there, Mr. Clean waits in ambush on top of the bureau. Then she wakes up and takes Yoga exercises for a while. Then she checks out all my shoes on the floor of the closet. When she finally decides everything's okay, she slinks out of the closet and ZAP! Mr. Clean hits her with a flying tackle. They roll all over the floor pretending to claw each other to death. When Mr. Clean gets enough, he jumps up into my lap and tries to crawl inside my shirt the way he used to when he was little. Only trouble, he is getting too big, and he can't figure out why it's such a tight fit in there. He is a riot.

I nearly forgot. I have one good thing to report

about Science Fair Day. We had cherry pie at the cafeteria. You know me and cherry pie.

Write again when you have time. Tell the gang hi.

So long,
Loren

* * *

WILLOW VALLEY SCHOOL
NEWS
Science Fair a Success
by Pam Hawkins (6th Grade)

Willow Valley's annual Science Fair was held last Friday in the gym. Our parents came and a lot of other people, too. More people came than last year, Mr. Wheeler said. A man came from the Canfield *Sentinel* and took pictures.

Some of the projects were as follows. Susan Ridley (6th grade) had a collection of kites to show how air currents work. Myra Gooder (4th grade) had a real baby alligator in a cage. She made a book that told what he ate and how alligators are part of the ecology.

Bob Stevens (6th grade) got the prize for best project. He made some stick men of wire. The stick men showed when we use our muscles for things like walking, lifting, and throwing. There was red yarn to show the muscles. Bob Stevens is in Mrs. Ault's room.

* * *

April 22

Dear Mrs. Ault,

Will you please give me a written report on the events leading up to the disturbance on the playground at noon today?

Mr. Wheeler

* * *

Dear Mr. Wheeler,

I'll try to tell you more about the incident on the playground at noon Monday. As you know, Loren Ramsey entered school late. The other children had been working on their projects for the Science Fair since January. When I told Loren about the fair, he asked if he could exhibit a rock collection that he had already collected himself. I said yes.

Loren was very proud of this rock collection.

he wanted friends in class, he should do what they want to do instead of trying to get his own way so much. Also, he should not boast.

After I talked to Loren, he went to work on a new project. This was only about a week ago. The title he chose was "How the Buffalo Helped the Indians." I didn't expect very much. His record from his school in Oregon was excellent, but the work he has done in my class is only average. I rather suspect that he invented the rock collection story as a stall. He hoped to be excused from doing a science project altogether, but "woke up" too late and found out he was going to get a very poor grade instead.

To continue with the story, Loren finished the chart he planned to use for the background of his buffalo exhibit. It was well done. I praised him and showed it to the class. Unfortunately, the chart was ruined that same day when a jar of poster paint was spilled on it. I asked Loren how the accident happened, but he only sulked and refused to answer me. I now believe he spilled the paint himself and was ashamed to admit that he was so careless.

You may have noticed that Loren's project at the Science Fair was a very poorly done booklet on the buffalo. When we were putting away the science projects Monday morning, Bob and some of the other children had Loren's booklet. They were looking at it and laughing at it. Loren snatched the book away from them. I imagine the fight at noon grew out of this incident. Loren has a rebellious nature and bitterly resents being teased.

I am glad that Mr. Tuttle acted so quickly on the playground and separated the two boys before a real fight developed. Bob is bigger and stronger. I'm sure he would have given Loren even more to be rebellious about.

Helen Ault

April 14,
Willow Valley School

Mrs. Karen Ramsey
14 Melville Place
Canfield Heights, California
Dear Mrs. Ramsey:

It has been verified through witnesses that your son, Loren, started a fight on the school playground during the noon recess period, Monday, April 12. Since that time, I have tried to contact you by telephone, but have not found you at home. I am therefore notifying you by mail of the outcome of this incident.

Immediately following the encounter on Monday, Loren was brought to my office for disciplinary action. He is a new student and it was his first offense, so I did not punish him. I tried talking to him instead. I explained that fighting was not an acceptable solution to his problems and would not be tolerated. One of our educational goals at Willow Valley School is to develop habits of good sportsmanship and fair play in our boys and girls. Competitions such as the Science Fair help to develop those habits. They challenge our students to do their best work through independent study and provide a way of rewarding students who excel through extra effort. Loren's disappointment at not winning is no excuse for holding grudges against those who do better work than he does.

I am sorry to report that during my talk with Loren, he was sullen and uncooperative. I am asking for your help at home so that together we might encourage him to deal with his emotions in a more mature way.

If you could come to school to talk about Loren's problem, I believe much could be accomplished.

Yours truly,
Albert Wheeler, Principal

* * *

Dear Sis,

*How I wish you were here to talk to! I don't
know whether I should be angry or ashamed, and
at whom or of whom. We think we know our
children, but do we, really?*

*Loren started a fight at school. Can you believe
it? Loren! On top of that, the boy he fought was
Bob Stevens, the one Loren raved about when he
enrolled last month. "Bob Stevens is the great-
est!" Loren said then.*

*Loren has no explanation to offer about the
fight. Or at least the explanation he gave me didn't
explain anything. He shrugged and said the kids
at school don't like him.*

"Why not?"

"I don't know," he said.

"Have you tried being friendly with them?"

"Yes."

"Did you start the fight?" I asked.

He wouldn't look at me. "Yes and no."

Karen Ramsey

I tried a new tack. "What was the fight about?"

"I guess it was about the Science Fair."

"Didn't you say Bob Stevens won first prize?"

"Yes."

"I thought you liked Bob Stevens. Don't you like him any more?"

"No."

"Why not?"

"He's sneaky."

"How, 'sneaky?' "

"He's just sneaky." Then he said, "Look, Mom, I won't get in any more fights, okay? If it's all the same to you, I'd just as soon not talk about it." He turned away to hide the tears in his eyes, and I felt like a witch for hassling him.

I took yesterday afternoon off from the office and went to school to talk to Mr. Wheeler and Mrs. Ault, Loren's teacher. Both of them kept referring to Loren's "personality problem," and it made me so indignant it was all I could do to keep from snapping their heads off. They'd already made

up their minds that Loren was jealous of this Bob
Stevens. Jealous!

They had quite a bit to say about Bob Stevens.
I gather the kid is some kind of prodigy at Willow
Valley School. Popular, outstanding athlete,
school leader — a little hero that no one wants to
offend, certainly not his teacher or his principal.
They claim Loren sulks when Bob gets attention
and Loren doesn't. Mrs. Ault said, "If Loren can't
be first in everything the class does, he loses interest."

They were so convinced this was so and spoke
with such certainty that for a while they almost
had me believing it. But only almost. There were
too many facts about Loren that I knew to be
true. If he is inclined toward jealousy, why wasn't
he ever jealous of Mark? Mark won more honors
than Loren did, and they've been best friends for
years! And if Loren loses interest when he isn't
first in everything as Mrs. Ault insists, why did he
go on year after year helping with the school float
for the Christmas parade? Other children were

36

asked to ride on it, but never Loren. Not once. I could go on and on with instances like this.

I truly believe it was a waste of time going to school to talk about the situation with Mr. Wheeler and Mrs. Ault. They said I must "help Loren to be a good sport." I had to bite my tongue to keep from showing how angry that made me! I told them according to my definition of a good sport, Loren was one already. I said that maybe there was something wrong with my definition and asked them to give me their definition of a good sport. I was trying hard to be polite, but Mr. Wheeler caught the note of sarcasm and went into a song and dance about cooperative parents. When I left, there was still a veneer of friendliness, but it had worn very, very thin.

On the way home, I thought maybe I should withdraw Loren from Willow Valley School for the rest of the year and enter him in a private school next fall. But Loren wouldn't hear of it.

"They already think I'm some kind of freak over there," he said. "If I pull out now, how will they ever find out any different? I'm not going to run. I'm going to show they're wrong if it takes forever!" His voice was trembling, and he abruptly went to his room and closed the door.

. . . Whereupon I curled up on the sofa and had a good cry of my own. Sorry, I couldn't help it.

Sis, do you think I'm reacting to this situation like an overprotective mother? Maybe Loren has faults that can be clearly seen by others but not by me. Do you *think* Loren is the kind of youngster Mrs. Ault believes him to be? If so, I wish very much that you'd tell me so.

Please write soon. I'm worried sick.

Love,
Karen

* * *

April 20

Dear Mrs. Ault,

A pupil from your class, Loren Ramsey, talked
to me in the cafeteria yesterday. He said that in
the school he came from in Oregon, the primary
teachers used a few 5th and 6th grade pupils to
help out with their little folks from time to time.
He said he had done this work and would like to
do it again. He offered to cut his own lunch period
short and come work with my children.

Loren impressed me as a responsible youngster
with a lot of pep and enthusiasm. I would like to
use him these last few weeks of school, if it can
be worked out with you.

Marjorie Williams
2nd Grade Teacher

April 21

Dear Mrs. Williams,

I realize that a few schools are using older boys and girls to help with the younger ones, so Loren may not be "fibbing" about his school in Oregon. We thought about adopting such a plan here at Willow Valley School two years ago, but it wasn't practical.

As for releasing Loren to help you, I would be glad to, but I'm not sure he would be much help. He is so moody and irritable he has made nothing but enemies among the children in my room. He has pestered poor Bob Stevens to death with his big ideas and tall tales. I'm afraid Loren would create more problems for you than he would solve.

Helen Ault

Willow Valley School
Mrs. Ault's Room
April 24

Dear Mr. Wheeler,

Thank you for coming to
our room to make a speech
yesterday. It was a good
speech. We hope you will
come again sometime.

Yours truly,

Bob Stevens, president
Mrs. Ault's 6th Grade

* * *

45

(Notice written on chalkboard, Mrs. Ault's room)

DUE FRIDAY, ONE-PAGE WRITTEN COMPOSITION, "A FRIENDLY CLASSROOM," BASED ON MR. WHEELER'S TALK TO US YESTERDAY. SOME OF THESE WILL BE READ ALOUD IN CLASS.

FINAL DATE FOR ENTRIES FOR THE CHAMBER OF COMMERCE CONTEST IS MAY 10. TITLE OF THE ESSAY, "ECOLOGY AND OUR TOWN." CONTESTANTS WILL NEED THE CHAMBER OF COMMERCE BULLETIN, *Canfield Heights: Facts and Figures,* TO WRITE THE ESSAY. MRS. BROOKS REMINDS CONTESTANTS THAT OUR LIBRARY HAS ONLY ONE COPY OF THIS BOOK. EACH CONTESTANT WILL HAVE TO GET HIS INFORMATION QUICKLY AND RETURN THE BOOK FOR OTHERS TO USE. CONTESTANTS ARE AGAIN REMINDED THEY MUST DO THEIR OWN WORK. ANY EVIDENCE OF CHEATING WILL AUTOMATICALLY DISQUALIFY THE CONTESTANT.

* * *

April 30

Dear Mark,

When I wrote you last week I told you Mr. Wheeler was coming to make a speech to our class. The way it turned out, it wasn't really a speech. What it was, he pretended he was talking to everybody in the room, but was really making a string of nasty cracks about me. Like sometimes I sneak off to the library to get a little peace and to talk to Mrs. Brooks the librarian who is the only person around here who is halfway human. Mr. Wheeler had a long spiel about "sore losers who go off in a corner and sulk."

He had some other goodies. For instance, the kids never have let me play ball with them on the playground. Not since the first day I came here. They figured the playground was their private property, because they got there first. "Buzz off," they told me. Well there's a guy named Donnie Wheatley. Once he asked me to play on his team.

47

All the rest of that day and the next, Bob Stevens teased Donnie about his friend Pansy Ramsey. (That's me.) I don't know what happened exactly, but Donnie didn't get to be a team captain any more. I think it must have been because of me, because Donnie stayed away from me after that, and so did the other kids.

Old man Wheeler didn't miss a thing. Like once I made this chart and Mrs. Ault bragged on it to the class. An hour later I saw Bob Stevens turn over a jar of poster paint on it while Mrs. Ault was looking the other way. Before I could get across the room, Bob was up talking to Mrs. Ault. He must have told her I messed up the chart myself, because next thing she was chewing me out for being so clumsy! She wouldn't have believed me if I told her what really happened, so I just shut up about it.

Okay are you ready for this? Here comes old Wheeler, making a speech to the class about "Good Sportsmanship." Guess what he says. He

BOB STEVENS

says, "We have some poor sports in this class who have temper tantrums and ruin their own work out of spite. They act like babies, not like boys and girls who are growing up into young men and young women!"

I thought I'd come unglued when he said that. Man, I couldn't believe it!

And now comes the really weird part. Before old man Wheeler made his speech, at least the kids mostly let me alone. Not any more, man! I find a nasty note in my desk about every day. The one this morning said, "Go back to Oregon, Sore Loser," but that is nice compared to some of them. Around this place good sportsmanship means getting a guy down for the count and then kicking him as hard as you can. Some sportsmanship.

Man, this place is so bad you wouldn't believe it. I told you I was waiting for that Chamber of Commerce book in the library. Mrs. Brooks said Bob Stevens had it and turned it in, but then the book disappeared again. I found out what hap-

50

pened to it. Bob Stevens turned it in and then swiped it so nobody else could write their essays. One of the kids in class let it slip that Bob did the same thing last year when the essay topic was "Population Growth and Our Town." It's old Bob's way of thinning out the competition.

I almost forgot to tell you. Talking about written compositions, after Mr. Wheeler's talk, Mrs. Ault made us write a composition about how to have a friendly classroom. Ha-ha. She called on some of the kids to read theirs, but she didn't call on me. She didn't even ask me to turn mine in. I've had mine in my notebook since last Friday and decided to send it to you. Please give it to Miss Stewart for me. Tell her I appreciate the kind of room she always had, and I hope she never changes. Tell her since I came here I have sure learned a lot, all bad.

I hope you keep quiet about all this stuff. The gruesome details, I mean. I don't want it to get back to Mom. She's been talking about moving *back to Oregon on account of me not liking school. To tell you the truth, I would sure like to move back, but if she gives up her job here it will be a long time before another promotion comes along.*

Thanks for writing. It sure helps.

Your friend,
Loren

* * *

A FRIENDLY CLASSROOM

by

Loren Ramsey

A friendly classroom is something every kid wants. In a friendly classroom there are lots of kids to play with and talk to. Everybody likes everybody else.

In a friendly classroom, you can learn more. There are plenty of others in the room to help you if you need help. It is easier to do your school work. No one will laugh or play a joke on you because you are trying hard. You can relax and do your best work without worrying. If you do a good job, your friends will be glad about it. If somebody does better than you, that is nothing to be ashamed of. You dont' worry about it, but will try harder next time.

It takes two kinds of people to make a friendly classroom, good winners and good losers. Even if the losers aren't mad to begin with, they will get mad if the winners rub it in. They will get mad if the winners laugh and call them dumb or stupid. No matter how good a sport you are, you can't be a good loser if the winners gang up and fink on you, or if they tell lies to get you in trouble just for the fun of it. Losers can't be good sports all by themselves. For a friendly classroom, winners have to be good sports too.

* * *

May 7

Dear Sis,

    Mr. Clean is dead. Mr. Lutkin was watering the ivy in front of the building about noon when the accident happened, so he saw the whole thing. Melon-Head tried to get Mr. Clean to cross the street with her, but he wouldn't. Finally she caught him and tried to carry him across. Apparently she didn't see the truck coming. Mr. Lutkin didn't know if she dropped Mr. Clean or if he managed to wiggle loose. Anyway the truck hit him and killed him.

    Mr. Lutkin put Mr. Clean in a box and saved him for Loren. I'm awfully sorry he did that. It would have been so much better if he had just quietly disposed of him. When I got home, Loren was sitting on the sofa in the living room staring down at what was left of his pet.

    Later, Mr. Lutkin came by the apartment and

offered to help Loren bury Mr. Clean. They dug a grave under a tree in the alley, and we buried him there just a while ago.

Sis, Loren hasn't said a word. No tears, no anger at Mel, nothing. When I ask him questions, he stares at me as if trying to comprehend, then answers in monosyllables. For six weeks now, Loren has been depressed, but his cheerful spirits have always returned when letters from Mark arrived or when he played with the cats. Now Mr. Clean is dead and Mel has disappeared. It's as if Loren had disappeared, too, leaving behind this — thing, that walks and moves and looks like Loren, but isn't Loren at all.

He can't take it any more, Sis. This is the last straw. I'm going to talk to Mr. Anderson tomorrow about getting my old job back in Minton. We never should have moved.

Karen

* * *

(Note on bulletin board in Mrs. Ault's room)

Below is Bob's entry for the Chamber of Commerce essay contest. It was so good that I asked him to share it with us. Please turn the pages of the booklet carefully. We want to keep it "daisy fresh" for the contest.

I am sorry to learn that so few students from the room are entering the contest. Perhaps this excellent work of Bob's will challenge others to try.

Mrs. Ault

* * *

ECOLOGY AND OUR TOWN
by
Bob Stevens

Washed by the ocean, kissed by the sun, and sheltered by the surrounding mountains, the town of Canfield Heights enjoys an enviable climate. In addition to year-round resort weather, our schools are among the best in the state. Our light industry provides a high rate of employment. Our large percentage of retirees gives us a stable economy. There seems to be little to mar the utopia to be found in this pleasant spot.

Yet with so many favorable conditions to be seen all around us, trouble looms on the horizon. Ten years ago less than 8000 automobiles traveled the streets of Canfield Heights. The nearest freeway was four miles away. Since then, the number of automobiles has doubled and a six-lane highway skirts the outlying residential area. We have learned what smog is.

Page 1

Dear Mrs. Ault,

"I'm sending notices to all the teachers that the original library copy of *Canfield Heights: Facts and Figures* has mysteriously turned up again.

Please be sure to announce this. Many boys and girls decided not to enter because the book was not available. (I still don't understand where it could have disappeared to. Bob Stevens was in the library when I found it on top of a file back by the old magazines. He laughed and told me I had misplaced it myself, but I don't think so.)

Mrs. Brooks, Librarian

P.S. I believe Loren Ramsey said he still intended to write an essay. Please be sure he knows the book is now available. He has only two more days left before the deadline.

* * *

Mrs. Timothy Stevens
475 Willow Lane
Canfield Heights, California

Bob, the important thing on a contest essay like this is the opening paragraph. Be sure to butter up the judges. Try something like this...

Washed by the ocean, kissed by the sun, and sheltered by the surrounding mountains, the town of Canfield Heights enjoys an enviable climate. In addition to year-round resort weather, our schools are among the best in the state. Our light industry provides a high rate of employment. Our large percentage of retirees gives us a stable economy. There seems to be little to mar the utopia of this pleasant spot.

...Daddy will make an outline for you when he gets home tonight. He'll be glad it's only an essay this time and not more stick men!

60

WILLOW VALLEY SCHOOL
N E W S
Chamber of Commerce Contest Won by 6th Grader
by Henry Sinclair (6th Grade)

Loren Ramsey from Mrs. Ault's room won first place in the Chamber of Commerce Annual Essay Contest. The judges announced their decision last week. Mr. Ronald Hooper, Chamber of Commerce secretary, said, "Loren Ramsey clearly showed us how wrong we have been to think of our ecology problems in local terms. Our problems here in Canfield Heights do not begin or end at the borders of our town, and we must change our thinking and planning to avoid making serious mistakes. As Loren said in his essay, 'One town's solution may be another town's disaster.'"

Loren was the guest of honor at the Rotary Club on Friday. He read his essay out loud, and Mr. Hooper gave him the first-prize check for $50.

Other entries from Willow Valley School were Pam Hawkins, Melissa Steele, Hank Sinclair, Manny Alvarez, and Arthur Jacobsen. Last year's winner, Bob Stevens, did not enter this year.

* * *

Dear Mr. Wheeler,

You'll be interested to know I had a long chat over the phone last night with Bob Stevens' mother. She talked "a mile a minute" as she usually does. I thought she would explain why Bob withdrew his entry at the last minute, but she didn't. In fact, I believe she telephoned to find out if *I* had an explanation!

I'm so pleased that Loren was able to "pull a rabbit out of the hat." Incidentally, is it too late to change the program for the 6th grade graduation ceremony? Donnie Wheatley wants Loren to be his partner in the procession.

Helen Ault

Dear Mr. Wheeler,

I think you should know that Loren Ramsey gave me part of his prize money to order five more copies of the Chamber of Commerce book for the school library. He said if there were more copies, then maybe more boys and girls would enter the contest every year. Isn't there some way we can thank him officially for this nice gift?

Mrs. Brooks, Librarian

* * *

Saturday, 9:00 AM.

Bob dear — A boy named Loren Ramsey telephoned, but I didn't want to wake you. He left a number for you to call, 254-4671. He said something about coming to his house this afternoon to help Donny Wheatley build a model airplane.

I'm at the club playing bridge if you need me.

Mother

Dear Mark,

   It's been a long time since I wrote, and you're not going to believe everything that's happened.

   I better start with Mr. Clean. The night after he got run over, Mom and I had the biggest fight of all time. That was about two weeks ago. It was an Alphonse and Gaston thing. Mr. Clean's funeral brought it on, I guess.

   Mom made up her mind nothing was ever going to get any better for us here in Canfield Heights. She said she was going to talk to her boss, Mr. Anderson, at the office. She said she was going to ask for a transfer back to her old job at Minton. I said she wasn't going to do that. She said yes she was, too, because I was miserable here and she loved me. Before the fight was over things got pretty sloppy.

   While we were busy yelling and slobbering all over each other, old Melon-Head sneaked into the apartment. At least, I guess that's when she sneaked in. Later that night I noticed all of Mr. Clean's cat food had been eaten out of his bowl, but I didn't think anything about it. Next morning it was raining outside, and I had to hunt for my raincoat. I turned on the closet light and heard something moving in that old box of rags.

Well you'd never in ten zillion years guess what. There was old Mel looking as pleased as Santa Claus the day after Christmas. There in the box with her were eight icky brown blobs squirming around. Kittens! Can you beat it? Eight! No wonder she was so big!

They didn't have any eyes or ears and not much hair. Man, new kittens are sure awful looking. Only a mother could love them.

At first I was still so mad about Mr. Clean I was ready to dump Melon-Head and her family out in the rain. Mom wouldn't let me, though. Mom said they'd all die if we disturbed them. "We've had enough sadness without that," she said. Then she said maybe she wouldn't talk to Mr. Anderson just yet, since we'd have to put off moving back to

Minton for a few days anyway on account of the baby kittens. (Yea!)

Well I went to school in the rain that day, but I sure was mixed up. One minute I was glad about Mel's kittens putting off Mom's talk with Mr. Anderson and the next minute I was thinking about Mr. Clean in the wet ground with all that rain coming down. We wrapped a plastic sheet around him, but still it sure gave me the creeps just thinking about him.

Then I got to school and looked up on the bulletin board. Mrs. Ault had put up Bob Stevens's contest essay with her usual glowing tribute. I still hadn't gotten a chance at the Chamber of Commerce book in the library, and I hoped now that Super Kid had gotten the head start he wanted, he'd return it.

Sure enough, that same afternoon Mrs. Brooks sent word to the room that the book had "mysteriously turned up." Some mystery. Anyway, I stopped by after school and got it. I thought kids would be waiting in line, but they weren't.

I'd already written most of my contest essay so all I needed was a few statistics from the book. It was a good thing, too, because I couldn't concentrate. Every five minutes I had to stop and go look at Mel's kittens. After all, it was my closet where she had them, so I felt like a father in a way. Or at least like a landlord.

("Landlord" reminds me. In case you're wondering about Mr. Lutkin and his one-pet rule, I did, too, so I phoned him and told him. He wasn't mad though. He just laughed and said let him know when Mel was ready to put her babies up for adoption. He said he knew of a few happy homes that would love to have a kitten.)

But I'm not through telling you about that night.

You know how people sometimes forget and leave things in library books? Like letters or hairpins or sometimes even money? Well I came across this piece of stationery somebody had forgotten and left in the Chamber of Commerce book. It had a name and address printed up at the top and a lady's handwriting on it, only it wasn't a letter exactly. The printed name was Bob Stevens's mother and the address was where the Stevens live. What it was, Bob's mother had been writing what Bob should say in his contest essay. Worse than that, she'd written a remark farther down the page about wire stick-men, the project Bob entered in the Science Fair. It was all right there, plain as day. Bob Stevens's parents had been doing his school work for him!

I couldn't believe it. I had to read that sheet over two or three times before it would sink in. Man, did I ever have the goods on old Stevens!

So what was I going to do about it? I didn't know. Next morning I took the Chamber of Commerce book back to Mrs. Brooks, but I held onto the sheet. I went to our room and out of curiosity I checked it against Bob's contest essay that was still tacked up in the place of honor on the bulletin board. You guessed it. He'd copied what his mother wrote, word for word.

About that time something made me look

around, and there was Super Kid himself staring at that sheet of his mother's stationery. Man, it was pathetic. He looked like somebody trying to get up the nerve to jump from the twentieth floor of a burning building. I was enjoying every minute of it. In fact I was enjoying it so much I got ashamed of myself. I handed him his mother's sheet of stationery and told him, "You kept the book so long I guess you forgot about the incriminating evidence you left in it." By that time class was starting. Everybody was standing up to say the Pledge of Allegiance, so I walked away and left him.

Well, he was quieter than usual that morning. When I came back after lunch, his contest essay wasn't on the bulletin board any more. I don't know what happened to it and couldn't care less.

Are you still with me? This is sure getting to be a long letter. I'll try to speed it up.

On Friday I gave Mrs. Ault my contest essay all done up in a plastic folder with pretty graphs and maps. She got a funny look on her face. She said, "It looks like your entry is the only one from our room, Loren."

"What about Bob's?" I said.

"He asked me to return his essay," she said. "He said he'd changed his mind about entering the contest."

"Why?"

She shrugged and smiled. "I have no idea."

I believed her. She really didn't know why. What's more, I could tell it was bugging her. She likes having star pupils around that she can brag about in the teachers' lounge. Reflected glory, like.

I wasn't sure my essay was good enough to reflect much glory, but I had another idea that might brighten her day. I told her about Melon-Head and the kittens.

"They're too young right now," I said. "But if you want me to, I'll bring them to school next week."

Sure enough, she got that old gleam in her eye

and said that I should bring them.

And that's how it happened I cleaned out Mel's box.

See, the closet in my room is the biggest in the apartment. So when the moving van came that day with our furniture, Mom told the driver to put this box of rags in my closet with the Christmas ornaments and other stuff like that. Later we used rags out of the box when we cleaned, but nobody ever moved it. Mel came along and had her kittens in it and still nobody moved it. The first person to move that box was me.

Man was it heavy! I took the cat family out and still it was heavy. I dug down in the bottom (are you ready?) and there was my rock collection!

Man, I let out a whoop you could hear all over the block! I forgot all about Mel and the kittens and so did Mom. She helped me unpack the rocks. Every single piece was there — sandstone, shale, all six of those quartz samples, everything. Each specimen was wrapped in a separate piece of cloth. I sure didn't pack them that way and neither did

Mom, so one of the moving men must have done it. He'd put the wrapped-up rocks in the bottom third of the box, then filled in the top with rags he had left over.

Well, next day I mailed back the claim money to the moving van company and wrote Grandpa Ramsey that his Plymouth Rock chip wasn't lost after all. And on Monday, Mom helped me take the rock collection to school along with the cats. It was a very big deal. The kids drooled over the kittens, especially the girls, and all the kittens got spoken for, thank goodness. Donnie Wheatley said he'd help me deliver them after they're weaned.

School will be out in a couple of weeks. I asked Mom if I could have you come visit me, and she said yes. Donnie Wheatley and I are going to take life saving lessons at the Canfield Heights Community Center, and it would sure be fun if you could come, too.

Bob Stevens wants Donnie and me to go to Scout Camp with him in August, but I don't know. I don't mind being friendly with Super Kid, but I

73

don't know yet if I want to be all that *friendly*. I told Donnie I'd have to think about it.

Mom is going to write your mother. She says, is the 6th of June all right? We can meet you if you come down on the bus. Let me know soon. Donnie wants to meet you.

Chow old buddy,
Loren

* * *

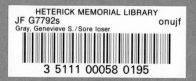